OTIS LEMON
AND THE MAGIC SCOOTER

By Mark Lemon
Illustrated By Maia Walczak

Published by Lemon Drop books

This is a story about an ordinary boy called Otis Lemon. He has a magical story to tell, which he would like to share with you all.

Otis Lemon lives with his Mum and Dad in a large city called Bristol. Otis is an ordinary boy, in an ordinary world, but when he visits his Uncle, Professor Poopy, at his workshop, magical things start to happen.

Let me tell you a little bit about his Uncle, Professor Poopy. Professor Poopy wears a long, white coat, round spectacles and bright orange shoes.

He has long, messy hair and on some days it stands on end, resembling a disheveled peacock.

Professor Poopy is always working on exciting inventions. Only last week, he made a hot air balloon made with Mrs Poopy's bed sheets and an old bicycle. Unfortunately, the invention did not work very well

and Professor Poopy landed on his next-door neighbor's house and got stuck on the roof! Mrs Poopy was not very happy at all and made Professor Poopy wash the dirty dishes for a whole week!

Now let's get to the story, as there is an exciting story to tell.

It was a sunny autumn Wednesday afternoon,

and Otis had just finished his day at school.
Otis was making his way to his uncle's house
on his new, red BMX bicycle.

His uncle had sent Otis a message the night before, using his magical flying Poopy plane to tell him that he had a very special new invention to show him.

As always, the plane had come through Otis' window, circled the room, then dropped the message onto his bed.

The message read:
"Visit my workshop after school. If you like flying, you'll think this invention is super cool."

Otis arrived at his uncle's house, got out his key, unlocked the door and went inside.

"Uncle? Uncle, are you there?" shouted Otis.

"Yes, Otis! I'm outside my workshop, in the garden."

Otis went down the long, winding garden path to the workshop. Outside the workshop, he saw what looked like a colourful scooter but it had two rocket boosters attached to each side.

"This isn't just a normal scooter." Otis thought to himself.

"Ah, hello Otis. Thank you for coming," said Professor Poopy.

"What is this, Uncle?" asked Otis.

"This, my dear boy, is my new special invention - the Magic Scooter!"

"It looks amazing, Uncle, but what does it do?"

"Let me show you Otis, as I think it might be best if I try it out first," answered Professor Poopy excitedly.

Professor Poopy stepped onto the Magic Scooter, put on his large yellow flying goggles and pushed the big green button on the handlebar.

All of a sudden, the scooter zoomed up into the air; over the houses, above the park and children below and up into the clouds, then whizzed back down to number 10 Cherry Tree Road, landing safely back outside the workshop.

"That was AMAZING Uncle!" shouted Otis.
"Can I have a go please?"

Professor Poopy pulled off the goggles and
scratched his head.

"Hmm, I'm not sure Otis. I don't think it's quite ready yet," his uncle said.

"Oh please Uncle! That looked like so much fun."

Excited to share his new invention, Professor Poopy

nodded, went into his workshop and came out with his favorite toolbox. Professor Poopy pulled out some funny-looking tools and after a few tweaks here and there, Professor Poopy had finished fixing the Magic Scooter. Otis was ready to start his adventure.

Otis stepped onto the scooter with great excitement.

"Now Otis, all you have to do is the push the green button. Let's see what happens this time." Professor Poopy declared with a grin, handing the goggles to his nephew.

Otis pushed the green button and all of a sudden he flew up into the air, over the houses below then flew over his school and up into the clouds!

"Wooooooooweeeeeeee!" shouted Otis.

Up high in the sky, Otis went through a thick grey cloud. When he came out the other side, he could see a very large aeroplane and the passengers were all waving excitedly, so Otis waved back.

"Hello!" he shouted.

All of a sudden, the magic scooter started to zoom back down to the earth below, this time over London, the capital city of Great Britain.

Otis flew past Big Ben, around the Houses of Parliament, along the river Thames and under the London Bridge.

"Woohoo, this is AMAZING!" shouted Otis.

Otis flew past Buckingham Palace and waved at the Queen of England as she stood on her balcony.

It was the Queen's birthday and there were lots of people cheering and waving flags outside the Palace.

"Hello Otis!" said the Queen, waving at him.

"Hello, Your Majesty! Happy Birthday" replied Otis.

The magic scooter zoomed up into the clouds again.
Not long later, it flew down over Bristol and whizzed
back down to number 10 Cherry Tree Road.

"Uncle, that was an amazing adventure!" Otis said,
a little breathless as he took off the goggles.

"Otis, this is just the start of many wonderful adventures," said Professor Poopy with a large smile.

After a delicious cup of hot chocolate, Otis left his uncle's house and cycled home. When he reached his house, he walked up the garden path, and smelled the wonderful dinner waiting for him on the kitchen table.

"Otis, your dinner is ready," called his mum as he came through the door.

"Coming, Mum, I have so much to tell you about my day," said Otis, as he took off his coat and shoes.

"Yes, yes dear, but first you must eat your dinner, please."

That night, Otis went to bed dreaming of the magic scooter, his trip to London and his wonderful flying adventure.

This is one of many amazing adventures for Otis Lemon and his uncle, Professor Poopy.

Goodnight.

LEMON
DROP
BOOKS